W9-DGV-360

HORSING AROUND

Dressage

Summit Free Public Library

Penny Dowdy

Crabtree Publishing Company

www.crabtreebooks.com

Crabtree Publishing Company

www.crabtreebooks.com

Author: Penny Dowdy
Editor: Lynn Peppas
Proofreader: Crystal Sikkens
Editorial director: Kathy Middleton
Production coordinator: Katherine Berti
Prepress technician: Katherine Berti
Coordinating editor: Chester Fisher
Series editor: Sue Labella
Project manager: Kumar Kunal (Q2AMEDIA)
Art direction: Dibakar Acharjee (Q2AMEDIA)
Cover design: Tarang Saggar(Q2AMEDIA)
Design: Shruti Aggarwal (Q2AMEDIA)
Photo research: Ekta Sharma (Q2AMEDIA)
Reading consultant: Cecilia Minden, Ph.D.

Cover: Philesha Chandler and Ricardo compete in the Wellington Classic Dressage Challenge II in West Palm Beach, Florida.

Title page: A dressage rider trains with her coach.

Photographs:
Cover: Perry Correll/Shutterstock (main image), Emberiza/Shutterstock, Tischenko Irina/Shutterstock, P1: Bob Langrish (main image), Emberiza/Shutterstock, P4: Bob Langrish, P5: Krafft Angerer/Bongarts/ Getty Images, P6: Library of Congress, P7: U.S. Army, P8: Bob Langrish, P9(t): Bob Langrish, P9(b): Carol Mingst, P10: Bob Langrish, P11: Rex Features, P12: Bob Langrish, P13: Bob Langrish, P14: Terry Fincher/Getty Images, P15: Bob Langrish, P16: Juniors Bildarchiv/Alamy, P17: Julian Herbert/Getty Images, P18: Nancy Jaffer P19: Bob Langrish, P20: Sarah Salmela/ Istockphoto, P21: Anja Hild/Istockphoto, P22: Bob Langrish, P23: Bob Langrish, P25: John Rich/Istockphoto, P26: Andre Gravel/ Istockphoto, P27: Bob Langrish, P28: Tish Quirk, P29: Bobby Yip/Reuters, Folio Image: Wendy Kaveney Photography/Shutterstock

Library and Archives Canada Cataloguing in Publication

Dowdy, Penny
    Dressage / Penny Dowdy.

(Horsing around)
Includes index.
ISBN 978-0-7787-4978-3 (bound).--ISBN 978-0-7787-4994-3 (pbk.)

    1. Dressage--Juvenile literature. I. Title. II. Series: Horsing around (St. Catharines, Ont.)

SF309.5.D69 2009   j798.2'3   C2009-903738-6

Library of Congress Cataloging-in-Publication Data

Dowdy, Penny.
  Dressage / Penny Dowdy.
    p. cm. -- (Horsing around)
  Includes index.
  ISBN 978-0-7787-4994-3 (pbk. : alk. paper) -- ISBN 978-0-7787-4978-3 (reinforced library binding : alk. paper)
  1. Dressage--Juvenile literature. I. Title.

SF309.5.D69 2010
798.2'3--dc22

2009023638

Crabtree Publishing Company

www.crabtreebooks.com   1-800-387-7650

Copyright © **2010 CRABTREE PUBLISHING COMPANY.** All rights reserved. No part of this publication may be reproduced, stored in a retrieval system or be transmitted in any form or by any means, electronic, mechanical, photocopying, recording, or otherwise, without the prior written permission of Crabtree Publishing Company.

Published in Canada
Crabtree Publishing
616 Welland Ave.
St. Catharines, ON
L2M 5V6

Published in the United States
Crabtree Publishing
PMB16A
350 Fifth Ave., Suite 3308
New York, NY 10118

Published in the United Kingdom
Crabtree Publishing
Lorna House, Suite 3.03, Lorna Road
Hove, East Sussex, UK
BN3 3EL

Published in Australia
Crabtree Publishing
386 Mt. Alexander Rd.
Ascot Vale (Melbourne)
VIC 3032

3 9547 00325 1480

Contents

Chapter	Title	Page
1	Dressage 101	4
2	History of Dressage	6
3	The Best Breeds	8
4	Olympic Dreams	10
5	Other Competitions	12
6	Para Equestrians	14
7	Making the Moves	16
8	Freestyle	18
9	Dressage Horses	20
10	Dressage Riders	22
11	Equipment	24
12	Care and Handling	26
13	Dressage Superstars	28
	Facts and Figures	30
	Glossary and Index	32

1 Dressage 101

Humans and horses have worked together for thousands of years. The bonds between people and horses continue today. Many people enjoy different types of **equestrian** sports. These include racing, jumping, and long-distance riding.

Dressage (druh-SAZH) is one of the most graceful sports to compete in. The sport starts with simple moves as the horse and rider go through basic walks and turns. Then the moves get harder. The rider may tell the horse to change speed. Other commands are to switch feet or turn on a dime. Dressage is also an Olympic sport. It can be a contest by itself, or part of eventing. Eventing is a group of equestrian sports that includes dressage, show jumping, and cross-country.

The horse and rider should have balance and must move smoothly as they go.

Dressage riders are beautiful to watch.

A dressage horse's moves should be strong and exact. Most of all, it should look graceful.

A dressage winner must display the strength and precision of a model horse. A dressage rider makes it look as though the two ride together as one. Dressage looks like horse ballet!

The rider gives the horse silent **cues**. It can be hard to see these cues. The rider may make a small move in the saddle. This tells the horse to turn. A squeeze of the rider's legs can tell the horse to stop. The horse and rider must connect with each other very well.

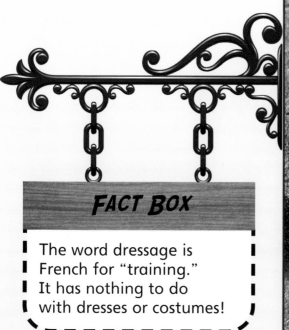

FACT BOX

The word dressage is French for "training." It has nothing to do with dresses or costumes!

This horse and rider won a dressage competition

5

2

History of Dressage

Dressage started long ago when **soldiers** trained their horses for battle. In battle, horses carried the soldiers and their weapons. Horses had to move exactly as soldiers trained them. A horse's ability to follow its rider's commands could mean life or death for a soldier!

In time, soldiers turned this training into a contest. These contests became very popular in Europe in the 1500s. The movements in these contests were called **Classical Dressage**.

In Classical Dressage, horses made most of the same movements we see today. One difference was the "airs above the ground" moves. In those moves, the horse jumped or stood on less than four legs. For example, in one move the horse hopped on its back legs while it held its front legs up in the air.

Dressage started as a competition among soldiers.

In another "air" move, the horse squatted on its back legs and stayed very still. Today, competitions no longer require "airs above the ground" movements.

Nobility in Europe trained with riding masters to learn Classical Dressage. This training could take years. When the horse and rider finally mastered the dressage skills, they rode in competitions. The rich and powerful would watch other rich and powerful people compete. The horses, lessons, and competitions were too expensive for common people to afford.

FACT BOX

The ancient Greek writer Xenophon, wrote *The Art of Horsemanship* in 322 B.C.

United States soldiers trained for dressage at Fort Riley.

The Best Breeds

3

All **breeds** are able to compete and perform well in dressage. Past competitions only allowed breeds that could perform "airs above the ground." Today, you may be surprised at the many breeds that compete.

Classical Dressage breeds include Lipizzans and Andalusians. These horses of Spanish origin, or heritage, can stand and jump on their back legs to perform "air" movements. They are both fast and light. This made them good for soldiers and for show. Royal families in Europe owned Lipizzans for hundreds of years. It is one of Europe's oldest breeds of horse.

Andalusians helped humans throughout history. They are even in 2,500-year-old cave paintings!

Lipizzaners can perform "airs above the ground" movements.

Andalusians were valuable in Europe. It was against the law to take them from the continent. The Andulusian didn't arrive in the United States until 1930.

Today's dressage breeds include Arabians, Quarter Horses, and Thoroughbreds. Arabians are smart and gentle. Their bodies give them both speed and **endurance**. Ranchers use Quarter Horses more than any other horse. This horse was named the "Quarter" Horse because it ran well in quarter-mile races.

The Dutch Warmblood is a common dressage horse.

Thoroughbreds came from England in the 1700s. Racing is their most common sport. Thoroughbreds compete in other sports that require exact movements.

This Arabian makes a great dressage horse.

FACT BOX

Dressage riders know Dutch Warmblood horses make great dressage horses. Some breeders raise these horses exclusively as dressage horses.

Olympic Dreams

Dressage became an Olympic sport in 1912. At that time, only soldiers were allowed to compete. When machines replaced horses in battle, dressage was no longer needed. Dressage did continue as a sport, however. Non-military riders began taking part after 1948. By 1952, the first women competed in Olympic dressage.

The 1912 Olympics started an important tradition. Up until 1912, no rule book or organization explained the contests for equestrian sports. This changed when the new equestrian sport called eventing was created. This sport is still part of the Olympics today. Eventing is one of the few sports where men and women can ride against each other.

The dressage rider and horse perform in the Olympic arena.

There have been some unusual Olympic game contests. In 1936, a 20-year-old rider competed against a 72-year-old rider.

Dressage was part of the 2008 Beijing Olympics.

In 1948, Sweden gave one of its best riders a **promotion** in the military so he could compete in the Olympics. Sweden won the gold medal. When word spread about this, Sweden took the promotion away. The rider's team returned the gold medal. The 2008 dressage event at the Olympics was one of the closest contests ever. American rider Steffen Peters missed winning a medal by just .00305 points!

FACT BOX

Olympic equestrian rules are set by the Fédération Equestre Internationale (FEI). The rules state the figures horses are tested on. They also explain which equipment is allowed. Riders must follow the rules. If they do not, they may lose points or be **disqualified**.

11

Other Competitions

In a dressage competition, the rider and horse perform tests and a freestyle event. The tests measure how well the rider and horse make certain movements, called figures. Judges score both the tests and freestyle with points of 0 to 10. Olympic judges also score events from 0 to 10. In the Olympics, the same riders compete in all events not just dressage.

The tests also show the gait of the horse. The gait is the way the horse moves. The figures show the judges many skills. The horse should create a rhythm as it moves, and look relaxed while doing it. The rhythm should move from front legs to back legs repeatedly. The horse and rider should move together, so the judges look to see that the rider does not have to pull the reins, or that the horse does not tug against the bit. Judges also look at the rider in the saddle.

The rider should be well-balanced, and use a shift in the saddle or small squeeze of the legs to signal the horse.

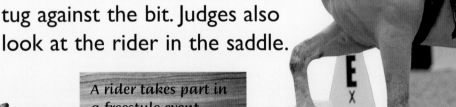

A rider takes part in a freestyle event.

A judge should notice very little motion when the rider makes these signals.

All tests must be completed in a set amount of time or the rider will lose points. All riders perform the same tests and in the same order. The Freestyle competition lets riders show off their horses in a more **artistic** way. The event is set to music. Half of the score is for how well the horse and rider perform the movements. The other half is for the artistry, or imagination of the performance.

The best riders also compete at the World Cup and the World Equestrian Games. The tests at these competitions have the toughest figures and judging. At the four earlier levels, riders and horses perform less difficult figures. The easiest figures and judging are at the training level. Most major countries have equestrian games. Even local horse clubs have events for beginning riders.

The dressage tests show how well the horse follows commands.

FACT BOX

Tests and scoring for beginning riders are less difficult. As riders and horses improve, the scoring and tests become harder. This gives beginners a chance to improve without being discouraged by low scores.

Para-Equestrians

People of all ages and abilities compete in dressage. This includes people with physical disabilities. Riders who can use approved equipment may compete in events for able-bodied athletes. Otherwise, they can compete in Para-Equestrian events.

Lis Hartel was one of the first four women to compete in dressage in the Olympics in 1952. When she was 23, she became sick with a disease called polio. The disease left her paralyzed below the knees. She could still ride, though! In the 1952 games, she won a silver medal. She used crutches to walk to the medal stand. In the 1970s, local horse clubs started holding contests for people who were disabled. Riders compete against people with similar disabilities. This makes the competition fair for the riders.

Lis Hartel won silver in dressage at the Olympics in 1952.

Para-equestrians adapt their equipment, such as this rider's saddle, to allow them to ride and compete.

Today, Paralympics is a world-wide event. FEI manages rules for para-equestrians just as they do for other major equestrian events. The FEI has also started holding dressage contests for riders of all levels. Riders with little use of their upper legs would not ride against people who could use their legs well.

FACT BOX

Para-equestrians can use special equipment. All equipment must be approved by judges. Adaptive equipment cannot give a rider an advantage over other riders. Special saddles help riders stay balanced if their legs are weak. Loops can help a rider hold the reins.

Making the Moves

In dressage competition a rider and horse complete a set of figures. Figures are similar to the required exercises that figure skaters complete. Keep reading to see how some basic figures should be performed.

Some movements are very simple. Judges score horses on how they walk. Horses must have rhythm— one, two, three, four—as they walk. They cannot drag their feet or move too fast.

When horses stop, it is called a halt. During a halt, the horse stands perfectly still, with its legs straight. Other movements are more complicated. For the rein back, the horse steps backward.

This horse steps backward in a rein back step.

Each step should be the same size. During a collection, the horse makes small steps forward, but raises its legs high. In an extended gait, a horse makes longer strides and keeps an even rhythm. It does not speed up.

During a half pass, the horse moves to the side. It steps leg over leg. At the same time, the horse must stand very straight, without twisting or bending. For the Piaffe, a horse stays in one place. It steps as high and evenly as possible. The Pirouette may be the hardest move of all. The horse steps sideways with its front legs to make a very tight circle.

Judges stand in different positions in the arena while the horse and rider complete their figures.

FACT BOX

A judge watches the rider and horse complete the figures. A scribe listens to the judge's comments and scores. Then the scribe writes them on an official form. Every judge has a scribe.

Freestyle

Freestyle is much newer than the other parts of the dressage competition. This competition, set to music, is sometimes called a kur. Here the rider and horse use the same figures, but they make it look more like a dance.

Freestyle shows the horse's personality. This makes the event exciting. Sometimes riders and horses wear costumes. This adds even more fun for the audience.

The freestyle lasts five minutes. As in the figures test, if the horse moves incorrectly, the judges remove points. If a beginner rider adds a difficult move, he could lose points or be disqualified. If a high-level rider leaves out a figure, the same could happen. The horse must walk, trot, and canter. This means its gait is slow, then medium, and then fast.

Costumed riders perform a pas de deux during a musical freestyle competition.

Most pieces of music do not change speed. So many riders use three different pieces of music. Riders choose music without words. This helps the audience pay attention to the horse and rider, not the words to the song.

Some dressage events include teams of riders. These teams perform in freestyle events with both horses making the exact same moves. The term pas de deux is French for "two steps." In dressage, pas de deux is freestyle with two riders and two horses. The word Quadrille includes "quad," which means "four." Quadrille is freestyle with four riders and horses.

FACT BOX

Many riders hire companies to design music and steps for them. The rider sends in a video of the horse's movements. The designer finds music that works well with the horse's own rhythm. Then the designer plans the movements to that music.

Four riders perform in a Quadrille.

Dressage Horses

Any horse can learn basic dressage movements. Riders lead horses through steps and movements similar to the figures in dressage tests. The rider starts with the simplest movements and focuses on rhythm and relaxation. As the horse improves, the rider adds new movements.

Young horses must start by getting used to people. This is an important step. Horses that are going to carry riders must be familiar with people. They need to let riders groom them and put equipment on them.

When a horse is able to carry a rider, training can begin. Even then, training should go slowly. A young horse should only be worked three or four days a week. Each training session should be about 45 minutes.

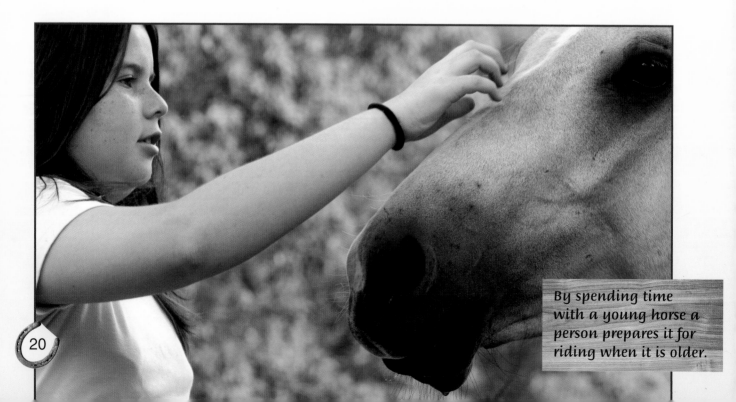

By spending time with a young horse a person prepares it for riding when it is older.

This helps prevent injury. It also lets the horse enjoy the workout. Training should not be a chore for the rider or the horse. Even the most experienced horses train only about an hour a day. As the horse gets more experience it may be ready to compete.

Beginning-level horses start with the simplest figures. The rider and horse can spend a year or more getting the simple figures perfect! As the horse gets better, it can go to harder competitions. Some horses compete for ten years or more.

This horse and rider practice about 45 minutes a day.

FACT BOX

Many dressage riders do not start with inexperienced horses. Instead, a rider may choose to buy a horse that has already been trained in dressage. This might cost at least $15,000!

10 Dressage Riders

The horse is not the only one that needs training. A rider must learn to guide the horse through perfect figures and give it the necessary commands.

Dressage riders do not ride yelling "Giddy-up" or "Whoa!" Instead, they give cues. These cues are slight body movements. A rider moves slightly in the saddle. He or she might squeeze a leg, or move a hand. These cues are all a horse needs to perform a figure correctly. To the audience, it looks like the horse and rider just know how to move together.

Riders learn one skill at a time. First, the rider learns the horse's beat as it walks, trots, and canters. The rider must work to keep the beat steady. Next, the rider learns to keep the horse relaxed and loose. Only then can the rider teach the horse commands through touch.

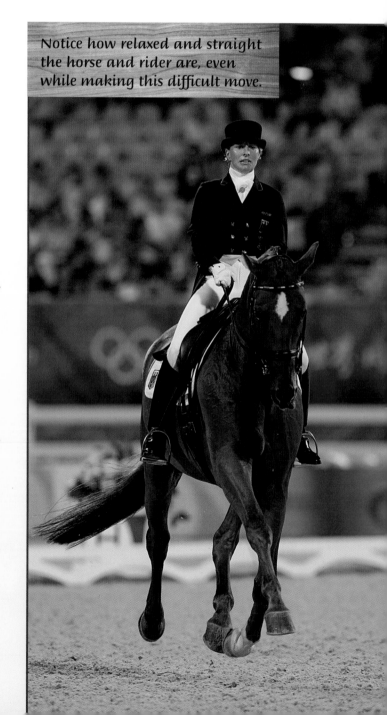

Notice how relaxed and straight the horse and rider are, even while making this difficult move.

Next, the rider works on movement. The horse should look like it enjoys moving. Most horses have a stronger or weaker leg. The rider must work to strengthen the weaker leg. Finally, the rider must be sure to show the horse's skills well. The horse does the work. The rider moves and corrects as needed.

FACT BOX

Dressage riders usually work with a coach. The coach watches the rider. He or she checks how the horse responds. Every time a coach and rider work with a new horse, they teach the skills, one at a time.

A coach instructs the rider on how to control the horse.

Equipment

Both the rider and the horse use special equipment. Some of the equipment keeps the rider or horse safe. Each competition has its own rules about what equipment is allowed.

Competition rules tell riders what to wear. Both men and women wear the pants, called breeches. These let the rider sit and move comfortably. On top, the rider wears a shirt, tie, and jacket. Some jackets look like men's suit jackets. A helmet protects a rider's head if he or she falls.

Some riders wear top hats to finish off the outfit. Other riders wear helmets. Some competitions require helmets.

The horse has equipment, too. A dressage saddle has a low, thin seat. This lets the rider sit close to the horse. It also lets the horse feel the rider moving in the seat. The bridle goes over the horse's head. The reins connect to the bridle and the bit. The bit is a piece of metal that fits into the horse's mouth. When the rider pulls the reins, it moves the bit. When this happens, the bit pushes on the horse's teeth, gums, or lips. This gets the horse's attention! Different dressage competitions allow different types of bits. The bits have names such as snaffles and bridoons.

helmet

bridle

jacket

FACT BOX

Dressage riders do not use whips on their horses like jockeys do with racehorses. Although dressage riders have spurs, they are not sharp. In dressage, riders communicate with horses using gentle touch.

saddle

breeches

reins

bit

Care and Handling

Dressage training and events are not hard on a horse. The moves are safe, and the events are not too long. This keeps the horse from becoming overtired or injured. A rider can also do many things to take care of a dressage horse.

Dressage horses need regular grooming. This starts with a good brushing from head to tail. The rider removes any dirt and knots. He or she checks the horse for any cuts. The hot breath of a horse can dry its lips and nostrils. Riders can use petroleum jelly to keep them moist. Riders can also use a special spray to get knots out of a horse's tail and mane.

Daily exercise includes a warm up, a work out, and a cool down. After a ride, the horse should be hosed down or sponged off. This cools down the horse's muscles.

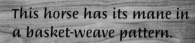
This horse has its mane in a basket-weave pattern.

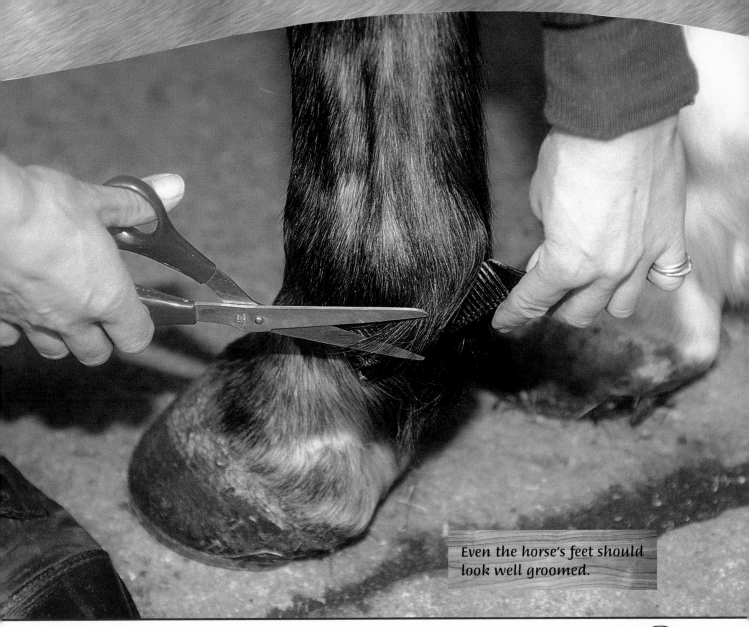

Even the horse's feet should look well groomed.

Many horses get a massage after a big workout. Just like with people, a massage makes the muscles feel good!

For shows, riders may dust horses with white coats in baby powder to look extra bright. They polish the coat to make it shine. Some riders put dark polish on the hoofs, too. Riders trim the horse's tail to look full and neat. A rider can even add a type of makeup to the horse's face!

FACT BOX

The rider can decorate the mane on a dressage horse. Bands of colored tape may match the rider's costume. Braids with pretty clips, ribbons, or beads can do the same thing.

Dressage Superstars

In the 1960s, only wealthy Europeans and Americans could afford dressage. A classical dressage breed could cost tens of thousands of dollars. California school teacher Hilda Gurney found a horse named Keen. Keen cost Gurney only $1,000!

Gurney and Keen trained wherever they could. They traveled across the country to clinics and horse clubs that offered dressage training. Everywhere they went people told Gurney that Keen would not perform as well as Classical Dressage horses. People also doubted a woman could train a horse for high-level competition. Gurney and Keen proved everyone wrong. Together they won five U.S. titles, gold and silver medals at two Pan American Games, and a bronze medal at the 1976 Summer Olympics.

Keen's former owners wanted him to become a successful racehorse. He never won. Gurney bought him for a cheap price.

Canadian Ashley Holzer's name frequently appears in the world's top ten rankings of dressage riders. Holzer competed in three Olympics, winning the bronze medal in 1988. Ten years later, the Toronto native and her horse, Pop Art, competed in the 2008 Olympic Games in Beijing, China. Though they did not win a medal, 2008 was still a great year. Holzer and Pop Art won every Grand Prix event they entered!

Holzer has competed with many horses. She started riding the Dutch Warmblood Pop Art when he was nine years old.

FACT BOX

If you want to become a superstar, find a college with a dressage team. Many college programs have teams with horses. This saves money while you get training and chances to compete! Mount Holyoke College in Massachusetts, for example, won the Intercollegiate Dressage Championship in four out of seven years.

Facts and Figures

Dressage competitions bring the grace and precision of the sport to the eyes of viewers. Here are some of the standout teams and individuals of the dressage world.

In Olympic competitions, the German team has dominated the sport, winning gold medals in every Olympics in the past 20 years. Many of the German team riders have earned individual Olympic medals, too. Isabell Werth and Nicole Uphoff have each won individual Olympic gold for Germany. Since dressage was added to the Olympic Games, Germany has won 18 gold medals.

Four riders have tied for the most Olympic medals in dressage: Reiner Klimke from Germany, Josef Neckermann from Germany, Isabell Werth from Germany, and Anky Van Grunsven from the Netherlands. Each of the riders won eight Olympic medals. Werth's horse, Gigolo, holds the record for most Olympic medals with six.

Maria-Paula Bernal is the youngest dressage rider to compete in the Olympics. The Colombian was only 16 when she rode in the 1988 Olympics. Austrian rider Arthur van Pongracz was 72 when he competed in the 1936 Olympics.

The FEI World Cup is held every year, but Germany has not been as dominant in this competition. While German Isabell Werth has won World Cup gold, so have American Steffan Peters and the Netherland's Anky Van Grunsven. As a matter of fact, Van Grunsven has won eight World Cups since 1995.

FEI World Cup Dressage Winners

2008–2009	Steffen Peters (USA) riding Ravel
2007–2008	Anky Van Grunsven (Netherlands) riding Ips Salinero
2006–2007	Isabell Werth (Germany) riding Warum Nicht
2005–2006	Anky Van Grunsven (Netherlands) riding Keltec Salinero
2004–2005	Anky Van Grunsven (Netherlands) riding Keltec Salinero

Competing in the Olympics is every athlete's dream. Dressage athletes are no exception. The highest honor is the gold medal, but the medal is all the rider gets for an Olympic win. There is no purse, or prize money, for winning the Olympics.

The FEI World Cup pays a hefty purse. Riders can earn more than $100,000 (U.S.) for a first-place win.

Other high-profile events, particularly in Europe, may pay large purses as well. For example, an event in Cannes, France, offers total prizes for all who place at nearly half a million dollars. Not all high-level competitions pay big prizes, however. The United States Dressage Federation (USDF) holds regional events for riders who want to qualify for the World Cup and the Olympics. A first-place win at a USDF regional competition may pay as little as $314 in prize money, a jacket, and an embroidered cooler.

Glossary

artistic Something that shows skill or imagination

breeds Certain kinds of an animal

Classical Dressage Equestrian sport with precise movements and airs above the ground

cues Signals

disqualified Removed from a contest

endurance The ability to last in a strenuous activity

equestrian Related to horses

nobility A important group of people belonging to a higher class

promotion Moving up in a job or position

soldiers People serving in the army or other military service

Index

"airs above the ground" 6, 7

Andalusians 8, 9

Arabians 9

Classical Dressage 6, 7

Eventing 4, 10

Fédération Equestre Internationale (FEI) 11, 15, 30, 31

figures 11, 12, 13, 16, 17, 18, 20, 21, 22

freestyle 12, 18–19

Gurney, Hilda 28

Hartel, Lis 14

Holzer, Ashley 29

Lipizzans 8

Olympic 4, 10, 11, 12, 14, 28, 29, 30, 31

para-equestrian events 14–15

pas de deux 18, 19

Peters, Steffen 11, 30, 31

Quadrille 19

Quarter Horses 9

soldiers 6, 7, 10

tests 12, 13, 18, 20

Thoroughbreds 9

Printed in the U.S.A.—CG

3 9547 00325 1480

FREE PUBLIC LIBRARY, SUMMIT, N.J.

APR   2010